HORRID HENRY

SPOOKY SPECTACULAR

FRANCESCA SIMON

FRANCESCA SIMON SPENT HER CHILDHOOD ON THE BEACH IN CALIFORNIA AND STARTED WRITING STORIES AT THE AGE OF EIGHT. SHE WROTE HER FIRST HORRID HENRY BOOK IN 1994. HORRID HENRY HAS GONE ON TO CONQUER THE GLOBE; HIS ADVENTURES HAVE SOLD MILLIONS OF COPIES WORLDWIDE.

FRANCESCA HAS WON THE CHILDREN'S BOOK OF THE YEAR AWARD AND IN 2009 WAS AWARDED A GOLD BLUE PETER BADGE. SHE WAS ALSO A TRUSTEE OF THE WORLD BOOK DAY CHARITY FOR SIX YEARS.

FRANCESCA LIVES IN NORTH LONDON WITH HER FAMILY.

WWW.FRANCESCASIMON.COM WWW.HORRIDHENRY.CO.UK @SIMON_FRANCESCA

TONY ROSS

TONY ROSS WAS BORN IN LONDON AND STUDIED AT THE LIVERPOOL SCHOOL OF ART AND DESIGN. HE HAS WORKED AS A CARTOONIST, A GRAPHIC DESIGNER, AN ADVERTISING ART DIRECTOR AND A UNIVERSITY LECTURER.

TONY IS ONE OF THE MOST POPULAR AND SUCCESSFUL CHILDREN'S ILLUSTRATORS OF ALL TIME, BEST KNOWN FOR ILLUSTRATING HORRID HENRY AND THE WORKS OF DAVID WALLIAMS, AS WELL AS HIS OWN HUGELY POPULAR SERIES, THE LITTLE PRINCESS. HE LIVES IN MACCLESFIELD.

HORRID HENRY

SPOOKY SPECTACULAR

FRANCESCA SIMON

ILLUSTRATED BY TONY ROSS

Orion

**Adult supervision is recommended when glue,
paint, scissors and other sharp points are in use.**

ORION CHILDREN'S BOOKS

Stories originally published in "Horrid Henry and the Secret Club", "Horrid
Henry's Revenge", "Horrid Henry's Stinkbomb", "Horrid Henry Wakes the Dead",
"Horrid Henry's Nightmare" and "Horrid Henry's Krazy Ketchup" respectively

This collection first published in Great Britain in 2019 by Hodder and Stoughton

1 3 5 7 9 10 8 6 4 2

A CIP catalogue record for this book is available from the British Library.

ISBN 978 1 51010 620 8

Printed and bound in Great Britain by Clays Ltd, Elcograf S.p.A.

The paper and board used in this book are from well-managed forests and other
responsible sources.

Orion Children's Books
An imprint of
Hachette Children's Group
Part of Hodder and Stoughton
Carmelite House
50 Victoria Embankment
London EC4Y 0DZ

An Hachette UK Company
www.hachette.co.uk
www.hachettechildrens.co.uk
www.horridhenry.co.uk

CONTENTS

PERFECT PETER'S

HORRiD DAY

"**HENRY**, use your fork!"
said Dad.

"*I'm* using my fork," said Peter.

"**HENRY**, sit down!" said Mum.

"*I'm* sitting down," said Peter.

"**HENRY**, stop **spitting**!" said Dad.

"*I'm* not spitting," said Peter.

"**HENRY**, chew with your mouth
shut!" said Mum.

"*I'm* chewing with my mouth shut,"
said Peter.

"**HENRY**, don't make a mess!" said
Dad.

"*I'm* not making a mess," said Peter.

"What?" said Mum.

Perfect Peter was not having a perfect day.

Mum and Dad are too busy yelling at **HENRY** all the time to notice how good *I* am, thought Peter.

When was the last time Mum and Dad had said,

"Marvellous, Peter, you're using your fork!"

"Wonderful, Peter, you're sitting down!"

"Superb, Peter, you're not spitting!"

"Fabulous, Peter, you're chewing

with your mouth shut!"

"Perfect, Peter, you never make a mess!"

Perfect Peter *dragged* himself upstairs.

Everyone just expects me to be perfect, thought Peter, as he wrote his Aunt Agnes a thank you note for the SUPER thermal vests. It's NOT fair.

From downstairs came the sound of raised voices.

"HENRY, get your muddy shoes off the sofa!" yelled Dad.

11

"**HENRY**, stop being so **HORRID!**" yelled Mum.

Then Perfect Peter started to think. What if *I* were **HORRID?** thought Peter.

Peter's mouth dropped open. What a **HORRID** thought! He looked around quickly, to see if anyone had noticed.

He was alone in his *immaculate* bedroom. No one would ever know he'd thought such a **terrible** thing.

But imagine being **HORRID**. No, that would never do.

Peter finished his letter, read a few pages of his favourite magazine, **Best Boy**, got into bed and turned off his light without being asked.

Imagine being **HORRID**.

What *if* I were **HORRID**, thought Peter. I wonder what would happen?

When Peter woke up the next morning, he did not dash downstairs to get breakfast ready. Instead, he LAZED in bed for an extra five minutes.

When he finally got out of bed

Peter did not straighten the duvet.

Nor did Peter **plump** his pillows.

Instead Peter looked at his 𝓉𝒾𝒹𝓎 bedroom and had a very **WICKED** thought.

Quickly, before he could change his mind, he took off his pyjama top and did not fold it neatly. Instead he **dropped** it on the floor.

Mum came in.

"Good morning, darling. You must be tired, sleeping in."

Peter hoped Mum would notice his UNTIDY room.

But Mum did not say anything.

"Notice anything, Mum?" said Peter.

Mum looked around.

"No," said Mum.

"Oh," said Peter.

"What?" said Mum.

"I haven't made my bed," said Peter.

"Clever you to remember it's washday," said Mum. She stripped the sheets and duvet cover, then *swooped* and picked up Peter's pyjama top.

"Thank you, dear," said Mum. She smiled and left.

Peter frowned. Clearly, he would need to work harder at being **HORRID**.

He looked at his *beautifully* arranged books.

"**NO!**" he gasped, as a dreadful thought sneaked into his head.

Then Peter squared his shoulders. Today was his **HORRID** day, and

HORRID he
would be. He went
up to his books
and knocked them
over.

"HENRY!"
bellowed Dad. "Get
up this minute!"

Henry **slumped**
past Peter's door.

Peter decided he
would call Henry
a **HORRID**
name.

"**Hello, Ugly**," said Peter. Then he went **WILD** and stuck out his tongue. Henry marched into Peter's bedroom. He glared at Peter. "What did you call me?" said Henry.

Peter **SCREAMED**.

Mum ran into the room.

"Stop being **HORRID**, Henry! Look what a mess you've made in here!"

"He called me **Ugly**," said Henry.

"Of course he didn't," said Mum.

"He did too," said Henry.

"**Peter** never calls people names," said Mum. "Now pick up those books you knocked over."

"I didn't knock them over," said Henry.

"Well, who did, then, the **man in the moon**?" said Mum.

Henry *pointed* at Peter.

"He did," said Henry.

"Did you, Peter?" asked Mum.

Peter wanted to be really really
HORRID and tell a **LIE**. But he
couldn't.

"I did it, Mum," said Peter. Boy,
would he get told off now.

"Don't be silly, of course you didn't,"
said Mum. "You're just saying that to
protect Henry."

Mum smiled at Peter and *frowned*
at Henry.

"Now leave Peter alone and get
dressed," said Mum.

"But it's the **WEEKEND**," said
Henry.

"So?" said Mum.

"But 𝒫ℯ𝓉ℯ𝓇'𝓈 not dressed."

"I'm sure he was just about to get
dressed before you **barged** in," said
Mum. "See? He's already taken his
pyjama top off."

"I DON'T WANT T° GET DRESSED,"
said Peter boldly.

"You poor boy,"
said Mum. "You
must be
feeling ill.

Pop back into bed and I'll bring your breakfast up. Just let me put some clean sheets on."

Perfect Peter *scowled* a tiny *scowl*. Clearly, he wasn't very good at being **HORRID** yet. He would have to try harder.

At lunch Peter ate pasta with his **fingers**. No one noticed.

Then Henry scooped up pasta with both fists and **SLURPED** some into his mouth.

"**HENRY!** Use your fork!" said Dad.

Peter **spat** into his plate.

"Peter, are you choking?" said Dad.

Henry spat across the table.

"Henry! Stop that disgusting **spitting** this instant!" said Mum.

Peter chewed with his mouth open.

"Peter, is there something wrong with your teeth?" asked Mum.

Henry **chomped** and **DRIBBLED** and **gulped** with his mouth as wide open as possible.

"**HENRY!** This is your last warning. **KEEP YOUR MOUTH SHUT WHEN YOU EAT!**" shouted Dad.

Peter did not understand. Why

didn't anyone notice how **HORRID**
he was? He stretched out his foot
and **kicked** Henry under the table.

Henry kicked him back harder.

Peter **SHRIEKED**.

Henry got told off. Peter got
dessert.

Perfect Peter did not know what
to do. No matter how hard he tried to
be **HORRID**, nothing seemed
to work.

"Now, boys," said Mum,
"Grandma is coming
for tea this afternoon.

Please keep the house tidy and leave the chocolates alone."

"What Chocolates?" said Henry.

"Never you mind," said Mum. "You'll have some when Grandma gets here."

Then Peter had a **TRULY** stupendously **HORRID** idea. He left the table without waiting to be excused and **sneaked** into the sitting room.

Peter searched high. Peter searched low. Then Peter found a large box of chocolates hidden behind some books.

Peter opened the box. Then he took a tiny bite out of every single chocolate. When he found good ones with GOOEY chocolate fudge centres he ate them. The YUCKY raspberry and strawberry and lemon creams he put back.

Hee Hee, thought Peter. He felt excited. What he had done was ~~ABSOLUTELY AWFUL~~. Mum and Dad were sure to notice.

Then Peter looked round the tidy sitting room. Why not **MESS** it up a bit?

Peter grabbed a cushion from the sofa. He was just about to fling it on the floor when he heard someone sneaking into the room.

"What are you doing?" said Henry.

"Nothing, **UGLY**," said Peter.

"Don't call me **UGLY**, **TOAD**," said Henry.

"Don't call me **TOAD**, **UGLY**," said Peter.

"**TOAD!**"

"**UGLY!**"

"**TOAD!**"

"**UGLY!**"

Mum and Dad ran in.

"Henry!" shouted Dad. "Stop being **HORRID!**"

"I'm not being **HORRID!**" said Henry. "*Peter* is calling me names."

Mum and Dad looked at each other.

What was going on?

"Don't lie, Henry," said Mum.

"I did call him a name, Mum," said Peter. "I called him UGLY because he is UGLY. So there."

Mum **STARED** at Peter.

Dad **STARED** at Peter.

Henry **STARED** at Peter.

"If Peter did call you a name, it's because you called him one first," said Mum. "Now leave Peter alone."

Mum and Dad left.

"Serves you right, Henry," said Peter.

"You're very strange today," said Henry.

"No I'm not," said Peter.

"Oh yes you are," said Henry. "You can't fool me. Listen, want to play a trick on Grandma?"

"No!" said Peter.

DING DONG.

"Grandma's here!" called Dad.

Mum, Dad, Henry, Peter and Grandma sat down together in the sitting room.

"Let me take your bag, Grandma," said Henry *sweetly*.

"Thank you, dear," said Grandma.

When no one was looking Henry took Grandma's glasses out of her bag and hid them behind Peter's cushion.

Mum and Dad passed around tea and home-made biscuits on the best china plates.

Peter sat on the edge of the sofa and held his breath. Any second now Mum would get out the box of half-eaten chocolates.

Mum stood up and got the box.

"Peter, would you like to pass round the chocolates?" said Mum.

"OK," said Peter. His knees felt WOBBLY. Everyone was about to find out what a **horrid** thing he had done.

Peter held out the box.

"Would you like a chocolate, Mum?" said Peter. His heart pounded.

"No thanks," said Mum.

"What about me?" said Henry.

"Would you like a chocolate, Dad?" said Peter. His hands Shook.

"No thanks," said Dad.

"What about me!" said Henry.

"SHH, Henry," said Mum. "Don't be so rude."

"Would you like a chocolate, Grandma?" said Peter.

There was NO escape now.

Grandma loved chocolates.

"Yes, please!" said Grandma. She peered closely into the box. "Let me

see, what shall I choose? Now, where are my specs?"

Grandma reached into her bag and **fumbled** about.

"That's funny," said Grandma. "I was sure I'd brought them. Never mind."

Grandma reached into the box, chose a chocolate and **popped** it into her mouth.

"Oh," said Grandma. "Strawberry cream. Go on, Peter, have a chocolate."

"No thanks," said Peter.

"**WHAT ABOUT ME!**" screamed
Horrid Henry.

"None for you," said Dad. "That's
not how you ask."

Peter *gritted* his teeth. If no one
was going to notice the chewed
chocolates he'd have to do it himself.

"**I WILL HAVE A CHOCOLATE**," announced
Peter loudly. "Hey! Who's eaten all
the FUDGE ones? And who's taken
bites out of the rest?"

"**HENRY!**" yelled Mum. "I've
told you a million times to leave the
chocolates alone!"

"It wasn't me!" said Henry. "It was Peter!"

"Stop blaming *Peter*," said Dad. "You know he never eats sweets."

"It's not fair!" shrieked Henry. Then he **snatched** the box from Peter. "**I WANT SOME CHOCOLATES!**"

Peter snatched it back. The open box fell to the floor. Chocolates flew everywhere.

"HENRY, GO TO YOUR ROOM!" yelled Mum.

"IT'S NOT FAIR!" screeched Henry. "I'll get you for this, Peter!"

Then Horrid Henry ran out of the room, slamming the door behind him.

Grandma patted the sofa beside her. Peter sat down. He could not believe it. What did a boy have to do to get noticed?

"How's my best boy?" asked Grandma.

Peter sighed.

Grandma gave him a big hug. "You're the best boy in the world, Peter, did you know that?"

Peter glowed. Grandma was right! He **WAS** the best.

But wait. Today he was **HORRID**.

NO! He was perfect. His **HORRID** day was over.

He was much happier being *perfect*, anyway. Being **HORRID** was **HORRIBLE**.

I've had my **HORRID** day, thought Peter. Now I can be *perfect* again. What a marvellous idea. Peter smiled and leaned back against the cushion. **CRUNCH!**

"Oh dear," said Grandma. "That sounds like my specs. I wonder how they got there."

Mum looked at Peter.

Dad looked at Peter.

"IT WASN'T ME!" said Peter.

"Of course not," said Grandma.
"I must have dropped them. Silly me."

"Hmmmn," said Dad.

Perfect Peter ran into the kitchen
and looked about. Now that I'm
perfect again, what good deeds can
I do? he thought.

Then Peter noticed all the dirty
tea cups and plates piled up on the
worktop. He had never done the
washing up all by himself before.

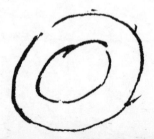

Mum and Dad would be so pleased.

Peter carefully washed and dried all the dishes.

Then he stacked them up and carried them to the cupboard.

"**BOOOOOOO!**" shrieked Horrid Henry, leaping out from behind the door.

Henry vanished.

Mum and Dad ran in.

The best china lay in pieces all over the floor.

"**PETER!!!**" yelled Mum and Dad.

"YOU **HORRID** BOY!" yelled Mum.

"**GO TO YOUR ROOM!**" yelled Dad.

"But . . . but . . ." gasped Peter.

"NO BUTS!" shouted Mum. "GO! Oh, my lovely dishes!"

Perfect Peter ran to his room.

"**AHHHHHHHHHHHHH!**" shrieked Peter.

SLAP!

"Waaaaaaaaaaa!"

SLAP! SLAP! PINCH!

"Muuuummmmmm!" shrieked Peter.
"Henry slapped me!"

"Did not!"

"Did too! And he pinched me!"

"Stop being **horrid**, Henry!" said
Mum.

"But Peter started it!" SHOUTED Henry.

"Did not!" WAILED Peter. "Henry did!"

Horrid Henry glared at Perfect Peter.
Perfect Peter glared at **Horrid Henry**.
Mum went back to writing her letter.

Horrid Henry **LASHED** out and **pulled** Peter's hair. He was a coiling cobra *unleashing his venom.*

"Eowwwwww!" shrieked Peter. **"GO TO YOUR ROOM, HENRY!"** screamed Dad. "I've had just about enough of you today!"

"FINE!" shouted Henry. "I hate you, Peter!" he shrieked, **stomping** up to his bedroom and **slamming** the door as loud as he could.

IT WAS SO UNFAIR! Peter was never sent to his room. Horrid Henry was sent to *his* so often he might as well live there full-time. Henry couldn't **burp** without Peter trying to get him into trouble.

"Mum! Henry's **DROPPING** peas on the floor!"

"Dad! Henry's SNEAKING sweets!"

"Mum! Henry's eating on the new sofa!"

"Dad! Henry's playing on the phone!"

Horrid Henry had had enough. He was **SICK AND TIRED** of that goody-goody ugly toad tattle-tale brat.

But what could he do about Peter? He'd tried selling him as a slave to Moody Margaret, but Henry didn't

think
she'd buy
him again.
If only he

knew how to cast *spells*, he could turn
Peter into a **toad** or a **BEETLE** or
a **worm**. Yes! Wouldn't that be great!
He'd charge everyone 10p to look at
his brother, **the worm**. And if Peter-
worm *ever wriggled* out of line he'd be
fish bait. **Horrid Henry** smiled.

Then he sighed. The truth was,
he was **stuck** with Peter. But if he
couldn't sell Peter, and he couldn't

turn Peter into a **worm**, he *could* get Peter into **trouble**.

Unfortunately, getting Perfect Peter into trouble was easier said than done. Peter never did anything wrong. Also, for some reason he didn't always trust Henry. The only way to get Peter into trouble was to **trick** him. And if it took all year, Horrid Henry vowed he would come up with a perfect plan. A plan to get Peter into trouble. **Big, big, BIG** trouble. That would be almost as good as turning him into a **worm**.

"I'll pay you back, Peter," **GROWLED**

Henry, **thumping** his teddy, **MR KILL**, against the bedpost. **"I WILL BE REVENGED ON YOU!"**

"What are you doing, Henry?" asked Peter.

"Nothing," said Horrid Henry.

Quickly he stopped **poking** around the old apple tree at the end of the garden and stood up.

"You're doing something, I know you are," said Peter.

"Whatever I'm **doing** is none of your business, *telltale*," said Henry.

"Have you found something?" said Peter. He looked at the base of the tree. "I don't see anything."

"Maybe," said Henry. "But I'm not telling you. You can't keep a secret."

"Yes I can," said Peter.

"And you're too young," said Henry.

"No I'm not," said Peter. "I'm a **big boy**. Mum said so."

"Well, too bad," said **Horrid Henry**. "Now **GO AWAY** and leave me alone. I'm doing something important."

Perfect Peter slunk off about ten paces, then turned and stood still, watching Henry.

Horrid Henry continued to **PROWL** around the tree, staring intently at the grass. Then he whistled and **DROPPED** to his knees.

"What have you found?" said Perfect Peter eagerly. *"Treasure?"*

"Much better than *treasure*," said

Horrid Henry. He picked something up and hid it in his hand.

"Oh show me," said Peter. "Please. Oh please!"

Horrid Henry considered.

"If — and I mean if — I tell you something, do you swear by the SACRED OATH OF THE PURPLE HAND to say nothing about this to anyone?"

"I swear," said Peter.

"Even if you're being tortured by aliens?"

"I WON'T TELL!" shrieked Peter.

Horrid Henry put his finger to his

lips, then tiptoed away from the tree to his fort. Peter followed.

"I don't want them to know I'm telling you," he WHISPERED, when they were hidden behind the branches. "Otherwise they'll disappear."

"Who?" whispered Peter.

"The fairies," said Henry.

"Fairies," squeaked Perfect Peter. "You mean you've seen—"

"Shh!" hissed Horrid Henry. "They'll run away if you tell anyone."

"I won't," said Perfect Peter. "Promise. Oh wow, fairies! In our garden! Oh,

Henry! Fairies! Just wait till I tell my teacher."

"**NO!**" screamed Horrid Henry. "Tell no one. Especially grown-ups. Fairies **HATE GROWN-UPS**. Grown-ups stink to fairies."

Perfect Peter clasped his hand over his mouth.

"Sorry, Henry," he said.

Horrid Henry opened his hand. It was sprinkled with *gold glitter*.

"*Fairy dust*," said Horrid Henry.

"It looks just like *glitter*," said Perfect Peter.

"Of course it looks like *glitter*," said Horrid Henry. "Where do you think *glitter* comes from?"

"*Wow*," said Peter. "I never knew *glitter* came from *fairies*."

"Well now you know," said Henry.

"Can I see them, Henry?" asked Peter. "**PLEASE** let me see them!"

"They only come out to *dance* at the

dead of night," said Horrid Henry.

"**Past my bedtime?**" said Perfect Peter.

"Course," said Horrid Henry. "**MIDNIGHT** is the **fairy** hour."

"Oh," said Peter. His face fell.

"Told you you were too young," said Henry.

"Wait," said Perfect Peter. "If they only come out at **MIDNIGHT**, how come *you've* seen them?"

"Because I've **SNEAKED** out and hidden up the apple tree," said **Horrid Henry**. "It's the only way."

"Ah," said Perfect Peter. "**Umm**," said

Perfect Peter. "Ooh," said Perfect Peter.

"I'm going to see them tonight," said Henry casually.

"Do you think you could ask them to come before seven thirty?" said Peter. **"OH YEAH, RIGHT,"** said Henry. "Hiya, fairies! My brother wants you to *dance* for him at seven o'clock." "SURE THING, HENRY," said Henry in a HIGH SQUEAKY fairy voice. "You don't speak to fairies. You have to hide up the tree. If they knew I'd seen them they'd run away and never come back."

Perfect Peter was in torment. He

wanted to see the 𝒻𝒶𝒾𝓇𝒾ℯ𝓈 more than anything in the world. But **getting out of bed** after lights out! And SNEAKING outside! And CLIMBING the tree! And on a 𝗌𝖼𝗁𝗈𝗈𝗅 𝗇𝗂𝗀𝗁𝗍! It was too much.

"I can't do it," WHISPERED Perfect Peter.

Henry shrugged. "Fine, baby. You need your rest."

Peter hated being called baby. Next to "smelly nappy", it was the **WORST** name Henry could call him.

"I am not a baby."

"Yes you are," said Henry. "Now go away, baby. Just don't blame me when you spend the rest of your life **moaning** that you missed seeing real live 𝒻𝒶𝒾𝓇𝒾𝑒𝓈."

Horrid Henry started to leave the fort.

Perfect Peter sat very still. 𝒻𝒶𝒾𝓇𝒾𝑒𝓈! But was he **BRAVE** enough, and **bad** enough, to SNEAK out of the house – at night?

"DON'T DO IT," whispered his angel.

"**DO IT**," squeaked his devil, a very small, sad, **puny creature** who spent his life inside Peter's head squashed flat by the angel.

"I'll come," said Perfect Peter.

YES! thought Horrid Henry.

"OK," said Henry.

Tiptoe. Tiptoe. Tiptoe.

Tiptoe. Tiptoe. Tiptoe.

Horrid Henry SNEAKED down the

stairs. Perfect Peter followed him. Softly, Henry opened the back door, and *slipped* outside. He held a small torch.

"**IT'S SO DARK!**" said Perfect Peter, staring into the shadows at the bottom of the garden.

"**Quiet**," whispered Horrid Henry. "Follow me."

They crept across the lawn down to the apple tree.

Perfect Peter looked up into the ghostly branches.

"It's too high for me to climb," he protested.

"No it isn't, I'll give you a leg up," said Horrid Henry. He **grabbed** Peter and *shoved* him up. Peter caught the lowest branch and started to climb.

"HIGHER," said Henry. "Go as **HIGH** as you can."

Peter *climbed*. And *climbed*. And *climbed*.

"This is **HIGH** enough," squeaked Perfect Peter. He settled himself on a branch, then cautiously looked down. "I DON'T SEE ANYTHING," he whispered.

There was no reply.

"Henry?" said Peter.

"Henry!" said Peter, a little louder.

Still there was no reply. Perfect Peter peered into the **DARKNESS**. Where could he be? Could Henry have been

kidnapped by *fairies*? **Oh no!**

Then Perfect Peter saw a **dreadful**
sight.

There was his brother, *darting* back
into the house!

Perfect Peter did not understand.
Why wasn't Henry waiting to see the
fairies? Why had he left Peter?

And then suddenly Peter
realised the **TERRIBLE** truth. His
treacherous brother had **tricked**
him.

"I'LL GET YOU – YOU'RE GONNA BE IN BIG TROUBLE –
I'LL – I'LL–" squeaked Peter. Then he

stopped. His legs were **too short** to reach the lower branch.

Perfect Peter couldn't climb down. He was **STUCK** up a tree, all alone, at night. He had three choices. He could wait and hope that Henry would come back and help him. **FAT CHANCE**. Or he could sleep all night in the **damp**, **COLD**, **scary**, **spooky** tree. Or he could—

"**MUUUUUUUM!**" screamed Peter. "**DAAAADD!**"

Mum and Dad **stumbled** out into the darkness. They were **FURIOUS**.

"What
are you doing
out here, Peter!"
SCREAMED Mum.
"You horrible boy!"
screamed Dad.

"It was Henry's fault!" shrieked
Peter, as Dad helped him down. "He
brought me here! He made me climb up."

"Henry is sound asleep in bed," said
Mum. "We checked on the way out."

"I am so disappointed in you, Peter,"
said Dad. "No stamp collecting for a
month."

"WAAAAAAAH!" wailed Peter.

"**SHUDDUP!**" screamed the neighbours. "We're trying to sleep."

Meanwhile, back in bed, **Horrid Henry** stretched and smiled. No one could pretend to be asleep better than Horrid Henry.

What a perfect revenge, he thought.
Peter in **TROUBLE**. Henry in the
clear. He was so excited he never
noticed his torn, **DIRTY**, **LEAFY**
pyjamas.

**Unfortunately, the next
morning, Mum did.**

HORRID HENRY'S

SLEEPOVER

Horrid Henry loved sleepovers. Midnight feasts! Pillow fights! Screaming and shouting! Rampaging till dawn!

The time he ate all the *ice cream* at Greedy Graham's and left the freezer door open! The time he jumped on all the beds at Dizzy Dave's and **BROKE** them all. And that time at Rude Ralph's when he — well, hmmn, perhaps better not mention that.

There was just one problem. No one would ever have **Horrid Henry**

at their house
for a sleepover
more than once.
Whenever Henry
went to sleep at a
friend's house, Mum

and Dad were sure to get
a call at three a.m. from a demented
parent SCREAMING at them to pick
up Henry immediately.

Horrid Henry couldn't understand
it. Parents were so fussy. Even the
parents of great kids like Rude
Ralph and Greedy Graham. Who

cares about a LITTLE noise? Or a **BROKEN**
bed? **Big deal**, thought Horrid Henry.

It was no **FUN** having friends
sleep over at *his* house. There was
no **RAMPAGING** and ｆｅａｓｔｉｎｇ at Henry's.
It was lights out as usual at nine
o'clock, no talking, no feasting,
NO FUN.

So when New Nick, who had just
joined Henry's class, invited Henry to
stay the night, Horrid Henry couldn't
believe his luck. New beds to **bounce**
on. New biscuit tins to raid. New
places to **RAMPAGE**. Bliss!

Henry packed his sleepover bag as fast as he could.

Mum came in. She looked GRUMPY.

"Got your pyjamas?" she asked.

Henry never needed pyjamas at sleepovers because he never went to bed.

"Got them," said Henry. Just not *with* him, he thought.

"Don't forget your toothbrush," said Mum.

"I won't," said **Horrid Henry**. He never *forgot* his toothbrush — he just chose not to bring it.

Dad came in. He looked even GRUMPIER.

"Don't forget your **COMB**," said Dad.

Horrid Henry looked at his **bulging** backpack stuffed with TOYS and COMICS. Sadly, there was no room for a **COMB**.

"I won't," lied Henry.

"I'm warning you, Henry," said Mum. "I want you to be on best behaviour tonight."

"Of course," said Horrid Henry.

"I don't want any phone calls at three a.m. from Nick's parents," said

77

Dad. "If I do, this will be your last sleepover ever. I mean it."

Nag nag nag.

"All right," said Horrid Henry.

DING DONG.

WOOF WOOF WOOF WOOF WOOF!

A woman opened the door. She was wearing a **Viking helmet** on her head and long *flowing* robes. Behind her stood a man in a velvet cloak holding

78

back five **ENORMOUS**, **SNARLING** black dogs.

"TRA LA LA BOOM-DY AY," boomed a dreadful, ear-splitting voice.

"**BRAVO, BRAVO!**" shouted a chorus from the sitting room.

GRRRRRRR! growled the dogs.

Horrid Henry hesitated. Did he have the right house? Was New Nick an **alien?**

"Oh don't mind us, dear, it's our opera club's karaoke night," trilled the Viking helmet.

"Nick!" bellowed the Cloak. "Your friend is here."

Nick appeared. Henry was glad to see he was **NOT** wearing a Viking helmet or a velvet cloak.

"Hi, Henry," said New Nick.

"Hi, Nick," said Horrid Henry.

A little girl toddled over, sucking her thumb.

"Henry, this is my sister, Lily," said Nick.

Lily *gazed* at **Horrid Henry**.

"I love you, Henwy," said Lisping Lily. "Will you marry with me?"

"NO!" said **Horrid Henry**.

Uggh. What a **REVOLTING** thought.

"Go away, Lily," said Nick.

Lily did not move.

"Come on, Nick, let's get out of here," said Henry. No **TODDLER** was going to spoil *his* fun. Now, what would he do first, **RAID** the kitchen, or **bounce** on the beds?

"Let's **RAID** the kitchen," said Henry.

"Great," said Nick.

"Got any good *sweets?*"
asked Henry.

"**Loads!**" said New Nick.

Yeah! thought **Horrid Henry**. His
sleepover **FUN** was beginning!

They sneaked into the kitchen. The
floor was covered with dog blankets,
overturned **food** bowls,
clumps of DOG HAIR and
gnawed dog bones. There
were a few suspicious-
looking PUDDLES.
Henry hoped they
were water.

"Here are the biscuits," said Nick.

Henry looked. Were those DOG HAIRS all over the jar?

"Uh, no thanks," said Henry. "How about some sweets?"

"Sure," said Nick. "Help yourself."

He handed Henry a bar of chocolate. YUMMY! Henry was about to take a **BIG BITE** when he stopped. Were those — teeth marks in the corner?

"**Raaa!**" A big black shape jumped on Henry, knocked him down, and snatched the chocolate.

Nick's dad burst in.

"Rigoletto! Give that back!" said
Nick's dad, *yanking* the chocolate out
of the dog's mouth.

"Sorry about that, Henry," he said,
offering it back to Henry.

"Uhh, maybe later," said Henry.

"Okay," said Nick's dad, putting
the **slobbery** chocolate back in the
cupboard.

Eeew, **gross**, thought Horrid
Henry.

"I love you, Henwy," came a lisping
voice behind him.

"AH HA HA HA HA HA HA HA!"

warbled a high, piercing voice from the sitting room.

Henry held his ears. Would the windows shatter?

"**Encore!**" shrieked the opera karaoke club.

"Will you marry with me?" asked Lisping Lily.

"Let's get out of here," said **Horrid Henry**.

Horrid Henry *leapt* on Nick's bed.

Yippee, thought Horrid Henry.

Time to get bouncing.

Bounce—
Crash!

The bed collapsed in a heap.

"What happened?" said Henry.
"I hardly did anything."

"Oh, I **BROKE** the bed ages ago,"
said Nick. "Dad said he was tired
of fixing it."

RATS, thought Henry. What a
lazy dad.

"How about a pillow fight?"
said Henry.

"No pillows," said Nick. "The dogs chewed them."

Hmmn.

They *could* sneak down and RAID the freezer, but for some reason Henry didn't really want to go back into that kitchen.

"I know!" said Henry. "Let's watch TV."

"Sure," said New Nick.

"Where is the TV?" said Henry.

"In the sitting room," said Nick.

"But — the KARAOKE," said Henry.

"Oh, they won't mind," said Nick. "They're used to noise in this house."

"DUM DUM DE DUM DUMM DUMM DUM DE DUM DUMM DUMM!"

Horrid Henry sat with his face *pressed* to the TV. He couldn't hear a word **Mutant Max** was shrieking with all that racket in the background.

"Maybe we should go to bed," said Horrid Henry, sighing.

Anything to get away from the noise.

"Okay," said New Nick.

Phew, thought Horrid Henry.
Peace at last.

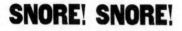

SNORE! SNORE!

Horrid Henry turned over in
his sleeping bag and tried to get
comfortable. He **HATED** sleeping
on the floor. He **HATED** sleeping
with the window open. He **HATED**
sleeping with the radio on. And he
HATED sleeping in the same room as

someone who **SNoRED**.

AWHOOOOOOO! howled the winter wind through the open window.

SNORE! SNORE!

"I'M JUST A LONESOME COWBOY, LOOKIN' FOR A LONESOME COWGIRL," blared the radio.

WOOF WOOF WOOF barked the dogs.

"**Yeowwww!**"
squealed Henry,
as five **wet**,
smelly dogs
pounced
on him.

"AWHOOOOOOO!"
howled the
wind.

SNORE! SNORE!

"TOREADOR – on guard!"
boomed the opera karaoke
downstairs.

Horrid Henry loved noise. But

93

this was *too much*.

He'd have to find somewhere else to sleep.

Horrid Henry *flung* open the bedroom door.

"I love you, Henwy," said Lisping Lily.

Slam! Horrid Henry shut the bedroom door.

Horrid Henry did not *move*.

Horrid Henry did not BREATHE.

Then he opened the door a fraction.

"Will you marry with me, Henwy?"

AAARRRGH!!!

Horrid Henry ran from the bedroom
and **barricaded** himself in the linen
cupboard. He settled down on a pile
of towels.

Phew. Safe at last.

"I want to give you a big kiss,
Henwy," came a little voice beside
him.

NOOOOOOO!

It was three a.m.

"TRA LA LA BOOM-DY AY!"

"-LONESOME COWBOY!"

SNORE! SNORE!

AWHOOOOOOOOOOOOO!

WOOF! WOOF! WOOF!

Horrid Henry crept to the hall phone and dialled his number.

Dad answered.

"I'm so sorry about Henry, do you want us to come and get him?" Dad mumbled.

"Yes," wailed Horrid Henry. "I need my rest!"

HORRID
HENRY
WAKING THE DEAD

"NO, NO, NO, NO, NO!"

shouted Miss Battle-Axe. "Spitting is not a talent, Graham. Violet, you can't do the can-can as your talent. Ralph, burping to the beat is not a talent."

She turned to Bert. "What's your talent?"

"I dunno," said Beefy Bert.

"And what about you, Steven?" said **MISS BATTLE-AXE** grimly.

"Caveman," grunted Stone-Age Steven. "Ugg!"

Horrid Henry had had enough.

"**ME NEXT!**" shrieked Horrid Henry.

"I've got a great talent! Me next!"

"**ME!**" shrieked MOODY MARGARET.

"**Me!**" shrieked Rude Ralph.

"No one who shouts out will be performing anything," said **MISS BATTLE-AXE**.

Next week was Horrid Henry's school talent show. But this wasn't an ordinary school talent show. Oh no.

This year was different. This year, the famous TV presenter **Sneering Simone** was choosing the winner.

But best and most **FANTASTIC** of all, the prize was a chance to appear on **Simone's** TV programme **TALENT TIGERS**. And from there . . . well, there was no end to the fame and fortune which awaited the winner.

Horrid Henry had to win. He just had to. A chance to be on **TV**! A chance for his *genius* to be recognised, at last.

The only problem was, he had so many talents it was impossible to pick just one. He could eat crisps *faster* than Greedy Graham. He could **burp** to the theme tune of Marvin the Maniac.

He could stick out his tongue almost as far as MOODY MARGARET.

But brilliant as these talents were, perhaps they weren't quite special enough to win. Hmmmm . . .

Wait, he had it.

He could perform his new rap, "I have an ugly brother, ick ick ick, a smelly toad brother, who makes me sick." That would be sure to get him on **TALENT TIGERS**.

"Margaret!" barked **MISS BATTLE-AXE**. "What's your talent?"

"Susan and I are doing a rap," said **MOODY MARGARET**.

what?

"I'm doing a rap," howled Henry.

How dare Margaret steal his idea!

"Only one person can do a rap," said **MISS BATTLE-AXE** firmly.

"Unfair!" shrieked Horrid Henry.

"Be quiet, Henry," said Miss Battle-Axe.

MOODY MARGARET stuck out her tongue at Horrid Henry. "Nah nah ne nah nah."

Horrid Henry stuck out his tongue at **MOODY MARGARET**. **AAAARRGH**! It was so unfair.

"I'm doing a hundred push-ups," said Aerobic Al.

"I'm playing the drums," said Jazzy Jim.

"**I WANT TO DO A RAP!**" howled Horrid Henry. "Mine's much better than hers!"

"You have to do something else or not take part," said **MISS BATTLE-AXE**, consulting her list.

Not take part? Was **MISS BATTLE-AXE** out of her mind? Had all those years working on a chain gang done her in?

Miss Battle-Axe stood in front of Henry, **baring her fangs**. Her pen TAPPED impatiently on her notebook.

"Last chance, Henry. List closes in ten seconds . . ."

What to do, what to do?

"I'll do *magic*," said Horrid Henry. How hard could it be to do some magic? He wasn't a **master of disguise** and the FEARLESS LEADER OF THE PURPLE HAND GANG for nothing. In fact, not only would he do *magic*, he would do the **greatest magic trick** the world had ever seen. No rabbits out

106

of a hat. No flowers out of a cane.
No sawing a girl in half — though if
Margaret volunteered Henry would
be very happy to oblige.

No! He, Henry, *Il Stupendioso*, the
greatest magician ever, would . . .
would . . . he would **wake the dead**.

WOW. That was much cooler than
a rap. He could see it now. He would
chant his **magic** spells and **wave** his
magic wand, until slowly, slowly,

slowly, out of the coffin the BONY body
would rise, sending the audience
SCREAMING out of the hall!

Yes! thought Horrid Henry,
TALENT TIGERS here I come.
All he needed was an assistant.

Unfortunately, no one in his class
wanted to assist him.

"Are you crazy?" said Gorgeous
Gurinder.

"I've got a much better talent than
that. No way," said Clever Clare.

"**Wake the dead?**" gasped Weepy William. "Nooooo."

RATS, thought **Horrid Henry**. For his **SPECTACULAR** trick to work, an assistant was essential. Henry hated working with other children, but sometimes it couldn't be helped. Was there anyone he knew who would do exactly as they were told? Someone who would obey his every order? Hmmm. Perhaps there was a certain someone who would even pay for the *privilege* of being in his show.

Perfect Peter was busy emptying
the dishwasher without being asked.

"Peter," said Henry sweetly, "how
much would you pay me if I let you
be in my MAGIC show?"

Perfect Peter couldn't believe his
ears. Henry was asking him to be in
his show. Peter had always wanted
to be in a show. And now Henry was
actually asking him after he'd said
no a million times. It was a DREAM
come true. He'd pay anything.

"I've got £6.27 in my piggy bank,"
said Peter eagerly.

Horrid Henry pretended to think.

"Done!" said Horrid Henry. "You can start by painting the coffin **BLACK**."

"Thank you, Henry," said Peter humbly, handing over the money.

TEE HEE, thought Horrid Henry, pocketing the loot.

Henry told Peter what he had to do. Peter's jaw **dropped**.

"And will my name be on the billboard so everyone will know I'm your assistant?" asked Peter.

"Of course," said Horrid Henry.

III

The great day arrived at last. Henry had practised and practised and practised. His MAGIC robes were ready. His MAGIC spells were ready. His coffin was ready. His props were ready. Even his DEAD body was as ready as it would ever be. Victory was his!

Henry and Peter stood backstage and PEEKED through the curtain as the audience charged into the hall. The school was buzzing. Parents *pushed* and **shoved** to get the best seats. There was a stir as Sneering Simone

swept in, taking her seat in the
front row.

"Would you please move?"
demanded Margaret's mother, waving
her camcorder. "I can't see my little
Maggie Muffin."

"And I can't see Al with your **big**
head in the way," snapped Aerobic

 Al's dad, shoving his camera in front of **MOODY MARGARET'S** mum.

"Parents, behave!" shouted Mrs Oddbod. "What an **EXCITING** programme we have for you today! You will be **AMAZED** at all the talents in this school. First Clare will recite Pi, which as you all know is the ratio of the circumference of a circle to the diameter, to 31 significant figures!"

"3.14159 26535 89793 23846

26433 83279," said Clever Clare.

Sneering Simone made a few notes.

"**Boring**," shouted Horrid Henry.
"Boring!"

"Shhh," hissed **MISS BATTLE-AXE**.
"Now, Gurinder, Linda, Fiona and Zoe
proudly present: the cushion dance!"

Gorgeous Gurinder, Lazy Linda,
Fiery Fiona and Zippy Zoe ran on
stage and placed a cushion in
each corner. Then they *skipped*
to each pillow, pretended to sew
it, then **hopped** around with a
pillow each, singing:

"We're the stitching queens
dressed in sateen,
we're full of beans,
see us preen,
as we steal . . . the . . . scene!"

Sneering Simone looked surprised.

TEE HEE, thought Horrid Henry
gleefully. If everyone's talents were
as ~~AWFUL~~ as that, he was a shoo-in
for **TALENT TIGERS**.

"Lovely," said Mrs Oddbod. "Just
lovely. And now we have William,
who will play the flute."

Weepy William put his mouth to

the flute and blew. There was no sound.

William stopped and stared at his flute. The mouth hole appeared to have vanished.

Everyone was looking at him. What could he do?

"TOOT TOOT TOOT," trilled William, pretending to blow. "TOOT TOOT TOOT-WAAAAAAH!" wailed William, bursting into tears and running offstage.

"Never mind," said Mrs Oddbod, "anyone could put the mouthpiece on upside down. And now we have . . ." Mrs Oddbod glanced at her paper, "a caveman **Ugga Ugg** dance."

Stone-Age Steven and Beefy Bert stomped on stage wearing leopard-skin costumes and carrying clubs.

"**UGGG!**" grunted Stone-Age Steven.

"**UGGG UGGG UGGG UGGG UGGG!** Me cave man!"

STOMP CLUMPA CLUMP
STOMP CLUMPA CLUMP
stomped Stone-Age Steven.

**STOMP
CLUMPA CLUMP
STOMP
CLUMPA CLUMP**

stomped Beefy Bert.

**"UGGA BUG
UGGA BUG UGG UGG UGG**,"

bellowed Steven, whacking the floor
with his club.

"Bert!" hissed **MISS BATTLE-AXE**. "This
isn't your talent! What are you doing
on stage?"

"I dunno," said Beefy Bert.

"BOO! BOOOOOO!" jeered Horrid

♫ ♫ ♫ ♫

Henry from backstage as the cavemen thudded off.

Then **MOODY MARGARET** and Sour Susan performed their rap:

"Mar-garet, ooh ooh oooh

Mar-garet, it's all true

Mar-garet, best of the best

Pick Margaret, and dump the rest."

RATS, thought **Horrid Henry**, glaring. My rap was so much better. What a waste. And why was the audience applauding?

"**BOOOOO!**" yelled Horrid Henry. "**BOOOOOO!**"

"Another sound out of you and you will not be performing," snapped **MISS BATTLE-AXE**.

"And now Soraya will be singing '*You broke my heart in thirty-nine pieces*', accompanied by her mother on the piano," said Mrs Oddbod hastily.

"Sing out, Soraya!" hissed her mother, pounding the piano and singing along.

"I'm singing as loud as I can," yelled Soraya.

BANG! BANG! BANG! BANG! BANG! BANG!

went the piano.

Then Jolly Josh began to saw "Twinkle twinkle little star" on his double bass.

Sneering Simone held her ears.

"We're next," said Horrid Henry, grabbing hold of his billboard and *whipping* off the cloth.

Perfect Peter stared at the billboard.

It read:

Il Stupendioso, world's greatest
magician, played by Henry

Magic by Henry
Costumes by Henry
Props by Henry
Sound by Henry
Written by Henry
Directed by Henry

"But Henry," said Peter, "where's my name?"

"Right here," said Horrid Henry, pointing.

On the back, in TINY letters, was written:

Assistant: Peter

"But no one will see that," said Peter.

Henry snorted.

"If I put your name on the front of the billboard, everyone would guess the trick," said Henry.

"No they wouldn't," said Peter.

Honestly, thought **Horrid Henry**, did any magician ever have such a **DREADFUL** helper?

"I'm the **STAR**," said Henry. "You're lucky you're even in my show. Now shut up and get in the coffin."

Perfect Peter was furious. That was just like Henry, to be so **MEAN**.

"**GET IN!**" ordered Henry.

Peter put on his skeleton mask and climbed into the coffin. He was fuming.

Henry had said he'd put his name on the billboard, and then he'd written it on the back. No one would know he was the assistant. No one.

The lights dimmed. Spooky music began to play.

"OOOOOOOOOOHHHH," moaned the ghostly sounds as Horrid Henry, wearing his special long black robes studded with stars and a special magician's hat, dragged his coffin through the curtains on to the stage.

"I am Il Stupendioso, the great and powerful magician!" intoned Henry.

"Now, *Il Stupendioso* will perform the greatest trick ever seen. Be prepared to marvel. Be prepared to be amazed. Be prepared not to believe your eyes. I, *Il Stupendioso*, will wake the dead!!"

"Ooohh," gasped the audience.

Horrid Henry swept back and forth across the stage, *waving* his wand and mumbling.

"First I will say the secret words of magic. Beware! Beware! Do not try this at home. Do not try this in a graveyard. Do not —" Henry's voice sank to a WHISPER — "do not try this unless you're prepared for the dead . . . to walk!" Horrid Henry ended his sentence with a **blood-curdling** SCREAM. The audience gasped.

Horrid Henry stood above the coffin and chanted:

"AbraCadabra,

flummery flax,

voodoo hoodoo

mumbo crax.

Rise and shine, corpse of mine!"

Then **Horrid Henry** whacked the
coffin once with his wand.

Slowly Perfect Peter poked a skeleton
hand out of the coffin,
then withdrew it.

"**OHHHH**," went the
audience.

Toddler Tom began to wail.

Horrid Henry repeated the spell.

"AbraCadabra,

flummery flax,

voodoo hoodoo

mumbo crax.

Rise and shine, bony swine!"

Then Horrid Henry *whacked* the coffin twice with his wand.

This time Perfect Peter slowly raised the plastic skull with a few tufts of blond hair glued to it, then lowered it back down.

Toddler Tom began to **HOWL**.

"And now, for the third and final time, I will say the magic spell, and before your eyes, the body will rise. Stand back . . ."

"Abracadabra, flummery flax,

voodoo hoodoo

mumbo crax.

Rise and shine, here is the sign!"

And **Horrid Henry** whacked the coffin three times with his wand.

The audience held its breath.

AND HELD IT.

AND HELD IT.

AND HELD IT.

"He's been dead a long time, maybe his hearing isn't so good," said Horrid Henry. "Rise and shine, here is the sign,"

shouted Henry, *whacking* the coffin furiously.

Again, nothing happened.

"Rise and shine, brother of mine," hissed Henry, **kicking** the coffin, "or you'll be sorry you were born."

I'm on strike, thought Perfect Peter. How dare Henry stick his name on the back of the billboard. And after all Peter's hard work!

Horrid Henry looked at the audience. The audience looked expectantly at Horrid Henry.

What could he do? Open the

coffin and *yank* the body out? Yell, "TA DA!" and run offstage? Do his famous elephant dance?

Horrid Henry took a deep breath.

"Now that's what I call DEAD," said Horrid Henry.

"This was a difficult decision," said **Sneering Simone**. Henry held his breath. He'd kill Peter later. Peter had finally risen from the coffin after Henry left the stage, then instead of slinking off, he'd actually said, "Hello

everyone! I'm alive!" and *waved*. Grrr. Well, Peter wouldn't have to pretend to be a **CORPSE** once Henry had finished with him.

". . . a very difficult decision. But I've decided that the winner is . . ." Please not Margaret, please not Margaret, prayed Henry. *Sneering Simone* consulted her notes, "The winner is the *Il Stupendioso*—"

"**YES!!**" screamed Horrid Henry, leaping to his feet. He'd done it! Fame at last! **HENRY SUPERSTAR** was born! Yes yes yes!

Sneering Simone glared. "As I was saying, the *Il Stupendioso* **CORPSE**. Great comic timing. Can someone tell me his name?"

Horrid Henry stopped dancing.

Huh?

What?

The **CORPSE?**

"**Is that me?**" said Peter. "**I won?**"

"**NOOOOOOOOO!**" shrieked Horrid Henry.

HORRID HENRY

AND THE REVENGE OF THE DEMON DINNER LADY

Horrid Henry crumpled up the paper and took aim.

There was the back of Margaret's head, so temptingly displayed in front of him. **TEE HEE**. Wouldn't she get a shock when a **big wet spitball** splatted her—

THWACK!

A dripping spitball *whacked* **Horrid Henry** on the neck. He turned round, glaring.

Who had **DARED** to spitball him during assembly? Rude Ralph was snickering. But so were Dizzy Dave and Brainy Brian. Well, just wait. Just wait. When he got his hands on—

"Settle down. Settle down, please," barked Mrs Oddbod. "Henry. Turn round and face the front. I have some important announcements."

Horrid Henry scowled. What could be more important than finding out who had **spitballed** him? That the infants would be practising their barn dance at playtime? That Perfect Peter was in the Good as Gold Book again? That **MISS BATTLE-AXE** was joining the circus? Now that, thought Horrid

138

Henry, would be an announcement worth hearing. Anything else — **BIG FAT YAWN**.

Mrs Oddbod gabbled on. "As you all know, this school is dedicated to healthy eating."

Oh no, not another lecture, thought **Horrid Henry**. If he heard the

horrible words vegetables, fruit and wholemeal bread again he would **SCREAM**.

"However" — she *glared* at Greedy Graham, Horrid Henry and Rude Ralph — "some of you appear not to know the meaning of the word *healthy*. Some of you keep bringing packed lunches to school filled with unhealthy, sugary snacks. A bar of **CHOCOLATE** is not a healthy meal."

Yummy, thought **Horrid Henry**. Three of his favourite words.

Sugar. Snacks. **CHOCOLATE**. He'd sneaked two bags of **Pickled Onion Monster Munch** into his Mutant Max lunchbox when Dad's back was turned. And he'd traded Bert an egg and cress sandwich for some **CHOCOLATE CRUNCHY CRACKLES**. Hmmm, boy, was he looking forward to lunchtime. He was sure he could pinch a pack of **Super Spicy Hedgehog** crisps from William when he was crying about something or other. And swap his raisins for Greedy Graham's **chocolate fudge**

bars. What a feast awaited him.

"Good job, Henry," burped his belly. "You sure know how to look after me."

"We've decided to appoint a lunchbox monitor, who will be checking every day and **confiscating** all unhealthy snacks," said Mrs Oddbod. "From today we will be a *sweet-free* school."

Huh?

Horrid Henry sat up. This did not sound good. In fact, this sounded **TERRIBLE**.

"I'm delighted to welcome back

142

an old friend to our school, someone who has been sorely missed. Children, please say hello to our new healthy food monitor – **Greta!**"

An enormous woman stood up and waddled over to Mrs Oddbod. Horrid Henry's blood turned to ice. It wasn't – it couldn't be – Greta.

Greasy Greta. Greasy Greta, the **Demon Dinner Lady!** That ape in an apron, that demon in dungarees, that sneaky sweet-snatcher, that **gobbling treat-grabber**. The last time Henry had seen **Greta** she'd run howling out of school after he'd spiked some biscuits with hot chilli powder. And now she was back ... **BIGGER** and **MEANER** and more **demonic** than ever.

Greasy Greta, a healthy food monitor? She'd *grab* all the treats for herself, and leave the carrots and celery sticks and wholemeal bread

behind. No one could sniff out sweets faster than Greasy Greta.

"I'll be checking all lunchboxes very thoroughly," said Greasy Greta. "**Very very** thoroughly. No sneaky sweets will escape me."

"Are there any questions?" said Mrs Oddbod.

Greedy Graham's hand shot up.

"What's going to happen to all the sweets?" he asked.

"All confiscated sweets will be given to charity," said Mrs Oddbod.

"That's right," said Greta. "All confiscated sweets will be safely disposed of." And she smiled her HORRIBLE greasy smile and flashed her *mouldy teeth*.

Yeah, down her gob, thought Horrid Henry mournfully. What a

job. Like putting a fox in charge of the rabbit hutches.

"Greta will also be giving healthy-eating talks," said Mrs Oddbod.

"Sweets are bad for you," said Greta. "I never touch them. Eat vegetables."

WHAT A LIAR, thought **Horrid Henry**. I'll bet she's never eaten a vegetable in her life.

But what to do? What to do? He couldn't face school lunches with **Sloppy Sally** sloshing food all over his tray. He wanted to keep his

packed lunch **AND** all his treats. But how? How? Somehow he'd have to find a way . . .

There was the rumbling, grumbling sound of a **dinosaur** approaching. Glasses shook. Trays trembled. Cutlery rattled. **Wobbling and gobbling**, Greasy Greta was on patrol.

"**GIMME THAT LUNCHBOX**," she thundered.

Greedy Graham *flung* his arms around his lunchbox, but he was no match for **Greasy Greta**.

SNATCH! *POP!*

Greedy Graham's lunchbox popped open. Greasy Greta emptied all the sweets and **FIZZY** drinks into her gigantic pockets.

"Next!" she bellowed.

Norwegian Norris tried to hide his treats in his pockets, but Greasy Greta's X-ray eyes spotted them.

"Hand them over," she barked, holding out her apron pockets.

"No," said Norwegian Norris.

"GIMME YOUR SWEETS!"

roared Greta.

Norwegian Norris obeyed.

"This wouldn't happen in Norway,"
he wailed.

Next up for
inspection was
Horrid Henry.

Greta towered
over him.

"Open your lunchbox," she ordered.

Henry opened the lid.

She'll never find my *sweets*, thought
Horrid Henry. He'd tucked his
CHOCOLATE FUDGE BARS up
his sleeves, leaving the carrot sticks
that he would be trading as soon as
he escaped.

Ha, ha, she'd never ever— Before

he could even finish that thought
Greta **snatched** his sleeves and shook
out his sweets into her **bulging**
pockets.

She was a **BLOODHOUND**.

Next up was Pasty Patsy. She
beamed at Greasy Greta. Greasy Greta
beamed at her.

"Run along, dear," said Greasy
Greta.

Huh?

"How come you didn't get inspected?" said Henry.

Pasty Patsy tossed her stringy hair and puffed out her MARSHMALLOW cheeks.

"'Cause she's my mum," said Pasty Patsy. "I can have anything I like for lunch."

Patsy snapped open her lunchbox, displaying rows and rows of sweets. Then she grabbed a handful and gulped them down.

"*Nah na ne nah nah*," smirked Pasty Patsy.

Horrid Henry's mouth watered.

IT WAS SO UNFAIR.

"Mum," said Henry that evening, "the **Demon Dinner Lady** is back and she's snatching our sweets."

"Good," said Mum. "You're not allowed to take *sweets* to school any more."

"But she's supposed to be the healthy-eating monitor and she's eating all the sweets herself."

"Glad to hear it," said Dad.

"**It's not fair**," wailed Henry.

Why did he have such **MEAN**, **HORRIBLE** parents? How could he live in a world with no sweets in school? He'd **DIE**. He'd SHRIVEL up into a little bit of thread and be blown away by the wind. He'd never be able to learn anything again, as all he'd be thinking about was sweets. He was doomed for ever to a lunchbox

of celery sticks and carrots and
brown bread sandwiches with crusts.

Oh, woe, woe, woe.

And then suddenly Horrid Henry
had a brilliant, SPECTACULAR
idea. It was so brilliant, and so
SPECTACULAR, and yet so simple,
that for a moment he could scarcely
breathe. He would set up in business.
The sweet-selling business. Who
better than Horrid Henry to ride to
the rescue of all his poor, starving,
suffering schoolmates whose MEAN,
HORRIBLE parents were obeying

the new no-sweets rule? He'd buy up loads of **CHOCOLATES** on his way to school, then sell them for twice the price in the morning break.

He'd be **rich!**

Business was brisk. Word spread through the playground that **HORRID HENRY'S TOP SECRET SWEET SHOP** was open in the Nature Reserve behind the climbing frame. Soon everyone's mouths were bulging with *sweets*

and treats, and Horrid Henry's pockets were **bulging** with cash. At this rate he'd be a *billionaire*, thought Horrid Henry happily. No, a *trillionaire*. No, a *gazillionaire*. And so long as everyone scoffed their sweets before Greta's inspection, she'd be left empty-handed. **The Demon Dinner Lady** would be defeated!

Tra-la-la. **Horrid Henry** sat on the bench counting his cash before the bell rang.

Oh, the *lovely, lovely sweets*. Oh, the lovely, lovely **MONEY**. Tomorrow he'd buy even more—

A **DARK**, **HIDEOUS** shadow fell across him.

Oh no. Help! **Greasy Greta** had sniffed him out.

Horrid Henry looked up, trying to hide all the unsold sweets filling his lap.

But it wasn't the *Demon Dinner Lady*. It was the head teacher, Mrs

Oddbod. She was on the warpath.

"Henry," she said. "Stand up at once."

Uh oh.

"How could you do this, Henry?" said Mrs Oddbod. "You know there are no sweets allowed in school."

"There aren't?" said Henry, trying to look as innocent as possible.

"Come with me. Those sweets will go straight into our charity cupboard."

"But . . . but . . ." spluttered Horrid Henry.

"No buts, you know the rules," said Mrs Oddbod.

Horrid Henry wanted to **SCREAM**. All his supplies. His lovely shop. His sweet-selling business, closed down before he'd made his first *million*.

Mrs Oddbod *marched* Horrid Henry down the hallway to the large storage cupboard. Every step spelled doom. Oh, my lovely **CHOCOLATES**, moaned Horrid Henry. Oh, my lovely money.

And he was in trouble. **BIG, BIG TROUBLE**.

"I am so disappointed in you, bringing sweets to school," said Mrs Oddbod, unlocking the cupboard. "And after all Greta's hard work, collecting sweets for charity," she added, *flinging* open the door, "I just don't know how you could—"

Greasy Greta stood in the cupboard

buried in *sweets*. Her face was smeared
with chocolate. So were her hands.
Sweet wrappers piled up around her.

"**GRETA!**" shrieked Mrs Oddbod.
"Is this how you set an example of
healthy eating?"

Greta's great **FISH** mouth gaped
open. And then closed. She *leapt*
out of the cupboard and pounded
down the hall, scattering sweets
everywhere.

"**You're fired!**" shouted Mrs
Oddbod after her.

Could those be the loveliest words
Horrid Henry had ever heard?

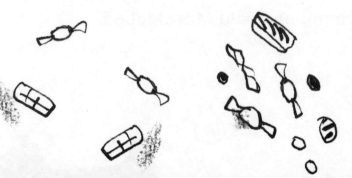

"That's what I was trying to tell you," said Horrid Henry. "I collected those sweets for charity and I was trying to hide them from her in the Nature Reserve when you found me. I knew she'd just eat them. You saw her."

That wasn't a lie. He was trying to hide the sweets from Greta. And the sweets were for his favourite charity, **CHILD IN NEED**. He was a child, and he was in need, so it was right that he benefit.

"Hmmmm," said Mrs Oddbod.

"Hmmmm. Well then, Henry, perhaps you would like to be the new healthy food monitor?"

"Me?" said Horrid Henry.

"You," said Mrs Oddbod.

Horrid Henry could not believe his ears. He'd never have to buy sweets again.

"Me inspect lunchboxes for sweets? I'd love to. I know all the hiding places, I can—"

"No," said Mrs Oddbod. "You'll lead by example. Only healthy food in your lunchbox from now on. Or else."

She glared at him.

"Oh," said Horrid Henry. "Rats." Goodbye chocolate, crips and sweets. Hello wholemeal bread and carrot sticks. Wah.

HORRID HENRY

AND THE REVENGE OF THE BOGEY BABYSITTER

"I challenge you to a name-calling competition," shrieked Rude Ralph. "For the title of champion name-caller of the universe."

HA, thought **Horrid Henry**. No one knew more rude names than Henry. Not even Rude Ralph.

"You're on," said Horrid Henry. "Woofy."

"Pongy."

"Smelly."

"Whiffy."

"Stinky."

"Reeky."

"Farty."

"Umm . . . Ummm . . ." said Ralph.

"Umm isn't a name," crowed Henry. "Nah na ne nah nah, I am champion."

"Shut up, I'm thinking," said Ralph.

"Poo breath."

"Gloppy goop."

"Smellovision."

"Odiferous."

"Odiferous?

That's not a word,"
said Ralph.

"Is too."

"Is not."

"Wibble pants."

"**Barf breath**."

"Turkey head."

"Turkey head?" said
Rude Ralph.
"Turkey head?
That's not a—"

DING DONG.

Horrid Henry stopped **jumping** up and down on Ralph's bed.

"Who's that?" said Henry.

Ralph shrugged. "We're having a **BABYSITTER** tonight," he said.

Horrid Henry's eyes gleamed.

A **BABYSITTER!** Yeah. What could be better than a sleepover at Ralph's with a **BABYSITTER?** He'd yet to meet one he couldn't tame. After all, he wasn't called the **Bulldozer of Babysitters** for nothing. A sitter meant hours of rampaging **FUN**. Especially as Ralph was bound to have one of those

brilliant **BABYSITTERS** who let you stay up all night and eat **biscuits** till you were sick and watch **SCARY** movies on TV. The kind his **mean**, **HORRIBLE** parents never ever got for him.

"Great," said Henry. "Who?" He hoped it would be Leafy Leon. He just sat with his headphones on doing his homework. Or Allergic Alice, who he'd heard was always too busy sneezing to see kids sneaking *sweets*. Or maybe — oh *please please please* — Dippy Dora.

Margaret said Dora had spent the whole evening on her phone and hadn't even noticed when Margaret stayed up past midnight and ate all the *ice cream* in the freezer.

"Dunno," said Ralph. "Mum didn't say. Probably Dora."

Yes! thought Horrid Henry.

"And Mum's baked a **chocolate fudge cake**," said Ralph.

"All for us?" said Henry.

"Nah," said Ralph. "Just a slice each."

Ralph looked at Henry.

Henry looked at Ralph.

"You thinking what I'm thinking?" said Henry.

"Oh yeah," said Ralph.

They could **GUZZLE** the whole cake and blame it on the BABYSITTER. What *brilliant* luck, thought **Horrid Henry**. Hmm boy, he could taste that yummy, **gooey** scrumptious chocolate cake already.

STOMP.

STOMP.

STOMP.

There was the sound of **elephants** trampling.

"What was that?" said Horrid Henry.

BOOM.

BOOM.

BOOM.

The **elephants** were joined by a herd of stampeding **RHINOCEROSES**.

"You don't think . . . " whispered Henry.

"It can't be . . ." whispered Ralph.

The walls sh**oo**k.

Henry gasped.

The ground sh**oo**k.

Ralph gulped.

"We'd better go and see," said Rude Ralph.

Henry and Ralph crept down the stairs and peeked round the door.

AAARRRGHHHHHH!

Stomping towards them was the **BIGGEST**, MEANEST, ugliest, **HIDEOUSLY HORRIBLE** teen Henry remembered from his worst nightmares. **Enormous** kid-mashing arms: check. **Enormous** spiky head: check. **Enormous** Henry-hating eyes and child-chewing fangs: check.

It was Rabid Rebecca, the **BOGEY BABYSITTER**, risen from the swamp where she thrashed around with the Loch Ness Monster and the Creature from the Black Lagoon.

"When you said you were having a

BABYSITTER, you never said it could
be — Rebecca," hissed Horrid Henry.

"I didn't know," whimpered Rude
Ralph.

"We're doomed," moaned Horrid
Henry.

"**WHERE'S THE FOOD?**" bellowed
Rabid Rebecca.

Ralph's mum
pointed to the
kitchen. "The
boys can
have a
SMALL

slice of cake each," she trilled. "Be good," she shouted over her shoulder as she escaped.

Then Rebecca saw Henry.

Henry saw Rebecca.

"**YOU**," said **Rabid Rebecca**. Her evil eyes narrowed.

"**Me,**" said Horrid Henry.

Last time he'd met **Rabid Rebecca** they'd had a fight almost to the death. Henry had hoped never to have a re-match. Then he remembered her weakness . . .

"Don't worry, she's scared of ***spiders***,"

whispered Henry. "All we have to do is find some—"

"And don't get any ideas about **spiders**," said Rebecca. "I brought my friend Rachel. Nothing scares her."

Horrid Henry gasped as a terrifying fiend cast a **BLACK SHADOW** over the sitting room. Rancid Rachel was even tougher-looking than **Rabid Rebecca**.

Rancid Rachel *glared* at Henry and Ralph. Her **fangs** gleamed.

"If I were you, I'd get straight upstairs to bed," growled Rachel.

"That way I won't step on you by mistake."

"But what about my chocolate cake?" squeaked Ralph. "My mum said—"

"**Our** cake, you mean," said the **BOGEY BABYSITTERS**.

"Don't you touch that cake!" squeaked Ralph.

"Yeah," said Horrid Henry. "Or else."

Rancid Rachel cracked her knuckles.

"Or else what?" she snarled.

Horrid Henry took a step back.

"Ooh, doesn't that cake look yummy," said Rachel. "Doncha think, Becs?"

"Yeah," said **Rabid Rebecca**. "I can't wait to eat it. Nice of the brat's mum to leave it all for us. Now go to bed before we **EAT** . . . YOU!"

"I'm not moving," said Horrid Henry.

"Yeah," said Rude Ralph. "Make me."

"GET OUT OF HERE!" boomed the bogey babysitters, exhaling their dragon breath.

Horrid Henry and Rude Ralph sat in his bedroom. They could hear the **BOGEY BABYSITTERS** cackling and laughing in the kitchen below.

"We've got to stop them stealing all the cake," said Ralph. "It's not fair."

"I know," said Henry.

"But how?" said Ralph. "She told us to stay in bed."

"So what," said **Horrid Henry**. He scowled. There had to be something they could do to stop the *crime of the century*.

"How?" said Ralph. "Call the police?"

Tempting, thought Horrid Henry. But somehow he didn't think the police would be too keen to race over and arrest two **HORRIBLE** babysitters for scoffing a cake.

"We could tell Rebecca it's poisoned," said Ralph.

"What, your mum made you a poisoned cake?" said Henry. "Don't think they'd believe you."

Rude Ralph hung his head.

"It's hopeless," said Ralph. "Now we won't get any."

No cake? No **YUMMY** chocolate cake dripping with fudgy frosting and studded with *sweets?*

Horrid Henry wasn't the **SQUISHER OF SITTERS** for nothing. Wasn't there some film he'd seen, or story he'd heard, where . . . where . . .

"Get some keys and some string," said Henry. "And one of your dad's suits on a hanger. Hurry."

"Why?" said Ralph.

"Do you want that cake or don't you?" said Henry. "Now do exactly what I say."

"AAAAARRGGGHHHH!"

The blood-curdling scream echoed through the house.

AAAAAARRRGGGGHHHHHHH!
AAAAAARRRGGGGHHHHHHH!
AAAAAARRRGGGGHHHHHHH!

Trudge.

   Trudge.

      Trudge.

Rabid Rebecca flung open Ralph's bedroom door. She *glared* at them screaming and trembling in the corner and flashed her **child-chewing** fangs.

"Stop screaming, you little creeps," snarled **Rabid Rebecca**. "Or I'll give you something to scream about."

"We saw . . . we saw . . ." gasped Ralph.

"A **headless ghost**," gasped Henry. "Outside the window."

Rabid Rebecca snorted.

"Yeah, right," she said. "Now shut up and go to sleep."

She left, slamming the door behind her.

"Go!" said Horrid Henry.

Horrid Henry ran into the kitchen, panting and gasping.

There were the **BOGEY BABYSITTERS**, huddled over the cake. One slice was already gone.

Rabid Rebecca looked up, cake knife in hand.

"I smell a child," she hissed.

"What are you doing down here?" roared Rancid Rachel. "Go away before we—"

"I'm **SCARED**," said Horrid Henry. "I heard a noise."

"You're just trying to make an

excuse to get out of bed, you little **worm**," said Rebecca.

"You'd better get out of here before I count to three," bellowed Rachel. **"OR ELSE."**

"There's something outside," said Henry.

"**ONE TWO THR—**"

Clink.

Clink.

Clink.

The clinking noise was coming from outside the kitchen window.

"There," whimpered Horrid Henry. He backed away.

"What was that?" said Rebecca, the cake halfway to her drooling jaws.

"Nothing," said Rachel, shoving a huge bit in her mouth.

Clink.

　　Clink.

　　　　Clink.

Rachel stopped chewing.

"That," hissed **Rabid Rebecca**. "That clinking noise."

"I told you there's something outside," whispered Horrid Henry.

BANG.

    BANG.

        BANG.

Rancid Rachel stood up.

"Ahh, it's just the wind," she said.

BANG.

    BANG.

        BANG.

"I'll show you," said Rachel. "I'm not scared."

She marched over to the window and drew back the curtain.

There in the dark was a headless suit, flapping and rapping at the window.

"**AAARRRGGGHHH!**"

screeched Rebecca. She spat out her mouthful.

"**AAARRRGGGHHH!**"

screeched Rachel. She spat out her mouthful.

"It's a **GHOST!** Hide!" they howled, racing from the kitchen and clambering up the stairs.

"Go outside and see what it is," screamed Horrid Henry.

"No way," shrieked Rebecca.

They barricaded themselves into the bathroom and locked the door.

Horrid Henry snatched the cake off the cake stand and *raced* back to Ralph's room.

Ralph was standing at the open window, dangling a hanger from a string with his dad's suit on it.

Henry beamed at
Ralph as he hauled in
the suit and untied the
keys he'd used to clink
on the ground.

Ralph beamed at Henry.

"Good job, partner," said
Henry, helping himself to a
gigantic piece of chocolate
cake. Hmmm boy, it was
delicious.

"Good job, partner," said
Ralph, digging into an even
BIGGER one.

"Won't your mum be furious with Rebecca when she comes home and finds all the cake gone?" mumbled Henry, taking another enormous slice.

"Boy will she ever," said Ralph. "I bet Rebecca never babysits here again."

HORRID HENRY'S

FEARSOME FUN

Turn the page for some bonus games and activities

Adult supervision is recommended when glue,
paint, scissors and other sharp points are in use.

Horrid Henry goes shopping!

HORRID HENRY IS DESPERATELY TRYING TO FILL HIS BAG WITH YUMMY TREATS, BUT HIS HORRIBLE, MEAN PARENTS KEEP PUTTING HEALTHY VEGETABLES IN IT! YUCK! CAN YOU SPOT THESE SIX ITEMS IN HIS BAG?

- ☐ CARROTS
- ☐ SMELLY SOCKS
- ☐ HOMEWORK
- ☐ CHOCOLATE
- ☐ SWEETS
- ☐ CRISPS

Trick or Treat

HENRY IS SO EXCITED ABOUT TRICK OR TREATING —
ESPECIALLY SCARING EVERYONE WITH HIS TERRIFYING
DEVIL COSTUME. CAN YOU SPOT THE DIFFERENCES IN
THE PICTURES BELOW?

I SPOTTED:

1 ☐ 2 ☐ 3 ☐ 4 ☐ 5 ☐ 6 ☐ 7 ☐

Wicked Wisecracks

HENRY LOVES HALLOWEEN! THE SWEETS, THE FILMS, THE COSTUMES . . . AND THE JOKES! HERE ARE A FEW OF HIS FAVOURITES:

Q: What do ghosts eat for supper?

A: Spooketti

Q: What is the most important subject a witch learns in school?

A: Spelling

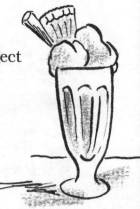

Q: What is a vampire's favourite fruit?

A: A nectarine!

Q: What kind of dessert does a ghost like?

A: I scream!

Q: What does a witch use to keep her hair up?

A: Scarespray!

Moody Margaret's Halloween Party

OH YES, FINALLY! MOODY MARGARET'S PARENTS ARE
LETTING HER THROW A HALLOWEEN PARTY.
IT'S GOING TO BE THE SPOOKIEST PARTY EVER.
HERE'S HOW TO MAKE SOME OF MARGARET'S SCARIEST
DECORATIONS:

HALLOWEEN GARLANDS

You will need:

Paper (the longer the better)

Scissors

Instructions:

1. Cut a long strip of paper

2. Repeatedly fold the paper back on itself

3. Draw something spooky on the front (bats, spiders, witches etc.)

4. Make sure the drawing goes to the edge on both sides so the chain is connected. You'll

need to leave part of the edge uncut.

5. Cut around your shape and unfold to reveal your spooky chain

HALLOWEEN LANTERN

You will need:

A stapler   A ruler

Glue   A pencil

Scissors

Paper

Instructions:

1. Fold a piece of paper lengthways and draw lines spaced about 3 cm apart. Make sure you leave a margin of 2 cm

2. Cut along the lines (starting on the fold)

3. Now unfold. Take one end and wrap it around to meet the other edge. Staple the top and bottom of the lantern

4. Use shapes cut out of paper to decorate the lanterns. You can make ghosts or pumpkins or anything you like!

5. Staple a strip of paper across the top to make a handle so you can hang your lantern

SNEAKY SPIDERS

You will need:

Pipe cleaners   Pom poms

String   Sticky tack

Instructions:

1. Cut eight pieces of pipe cleaner and stick them into the pom pom to make the spider's legs

2. Tie the spider to some string and secure to the ceiling with the sticky tack

3. Wait for them to scare unsuspecting party guests!

OF COURSE, A PARTY ISN'T A PARTY WITHOUT SOME
GREAT GAMES – AND MARGARET IS GOING TO HAVE
THE BEST AROUND!

TIN CAN TOSS

You will need:

Empty, clean tin cans, with the labels peeled off

Paint and brushes

Tissue paper

PVA glue

A tennis ball

Instructions:

1. Cover the tin cans with
   tissue paper using the PVA glue

2. Paint your cans. Make them as spooky as
   possible

3. Once your tins are dry, stack them and try to
   knock them all down with the ball

A MUMMY RACE

You will need:

At least four people

At least two rolls of toilet paper

Instructions:

1. Split into two teams. One person in each team will run the race

2. On 'Go', the other players wrap the runners in toilet paper as quickly as possible

3. When the toilet paper has run out, the runner can set off

4. The first person wrapped and across the finish line wins

PIN THE SPIDER ON THE WEB

You will need:

Lots of paper   Sticky tack

Markers   A blindfold

Instructions:

1. On a big sheet of paper, draw a web. You can make one out of string and stick it on if you prefer

2. Draw a spider for each player and cut it out. Write each player's name on the spider

3. Put a piece of sticky tack on the back of each spider

4. Take it in turns to be blindfolded. The un-blindfolded players spin the blindfolded player

5. Each player tries to get their spider as close to the middle of the web as possible. Whoever gets their spider closest wins

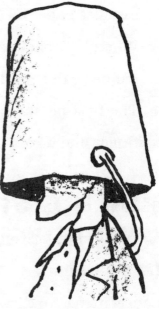

Halloween slime

HENRY LOVES HALLOWEEN AND HENRY LOVES SLIME –
BUT NOW HE HAS HALLOWEEN SLIME!
HERE'S HOW TO MAKE SOME:

You will need:

100ml PVA white glue (children's craft glue or
CE marked glue)

½ tsp bicarbonate of soda

Gel food colouring

Contact lens solution

Googly eyes or plastic insects

Instructions:

1. Mix the glue and bicarbonate of soda in a bowl

2. Add a few drops of food colouring. Green, purple or orange are all great Halloween colours

3. Add enough contact lens solution for your desired consistency and mix well

4. Add in your googly eyes to make monster slime or plastic insects for zombie guts slime

Dancing Ghost

HENRY HAS LEARNED AN INCREDIBLE TRICK TO IMPRESS HIS FRIENDS. TAKE A LOOK AT HOW TO MAKE A GHOST DANCE AND GET YOUR BOOGIE ON.

You will need:

A piece of tissue paper

A balloon

Scissors

Scary music (optional)

Instructions:

1. Cut a ghost shape out of tissue paper (about 5 cm long). Add some eyes if you'd like

2. Blow up and tie the balloon then quickly rub it on your hair for about 10 seconds

3. Slowly bring the balloon near the ghost and the ghost will begin to lift up towards the balloon

4. Move the balloon from side to side to make the ghost dance

Touch and Feel Boxes

THIS IS IT – HENRY HAS THOUGHT OF THE BEST HALLOWEEN IDEA EVER. HE'S MADE BOXES FULL OF HORRIBLE THINGS AND HE'S BET HIS CLASSMATES ONE WHOLE POUND THAT THEY CAN'T GUESS WHAT THEY ARE. A TRICK FOR HIS CLASSMATES AND A TREAT FOR HIM – WHAT COULD BE BETTER? TRY IT YOURSELF!

For all of these, you will need:

A box — tissue boxes, cereal boxes and shoe boxes all work well

Scissors — you'll need to cut a hole in each box big enough for a hand to reach into but small enough that you can't see what's in the box

Before you start, decorate the boxes to make

them spookier — use paint, pens or anything you can find.

Label each box with the scary 'items' inside.

HENRY'S TOUCH AND FEEL BOXES:

WHAT HENRY SAYS IS IN THE BOX	WHAT'S ACTUALLY IN THE BOX
Brains	Steamed cauliflower
Dried tongues	Dried apricots
Spiderwebs	Thread
Worms	Cooked, cold spaghetti
Eyeballs	Peeled grapes
Ears	Dried apple slices
Spiders' legs	Pipe cleaners
Teeth	Popcorn kernels
Witches' warts	Raisins
Maggots	Overcooked rice

Maze

MUM HAS DECIDED HENRY HAS HAD ENOUGH SWEETS AND HAS HIDDEN HIS TRICK OR TREAT BAG. CAN YOU HELP HENRY FIND IT?

Halloween Crafts

HENRY DOESN'T NORMALLY LIKE CRAFTS, BUT WHEN
THOSE CRAFTS INVOLVE MONSTERS, MUMMIES AND
SPIDER'S WEBS HE'S ALL IN. AFTER ALL, HALLOWEEN IS
THE BEST TIME OF THE YEAR!

GLITTERY SPIDERWEBS

You will need:

PVA glue

Glitter

A plastic sheet

Instructions:

1. Use the glue to draw a spider web on the plastic sheet

2. Coat in glitter

3. Leave to dry for at least 24 hours

4. Once dry, carefully peel the spiderweb off the sheet

MONSTER PUPPETS

You will need:

Paper bag

Acrylic paint

Coloured paper

Scissors

Glue

Instructions:

1. Paint the bag the colour of your choice —
   be sure to open it out to dry so that the sides
   don't stick together

2. Cut out shapes from
   the coloured paper
   to decorate — triangles
   for teeth, circles for spots, or
   whatever you want!

3. Once the bag is dry, use the glue to stick the
   shapes on and turn your bag into a monster

4. Stick your hand in the bag to use the puppet

STRING MUMMY

You will need:

Cardboard (black works best
but any colour will do)

White string

Googly eyes

Scissors

Tape

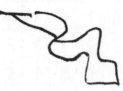

Instructions:

1. Cut a body shape out of the
   cardboard

2. Stick the googly eyes on to the head

3. Tape the string to the back of the
   mummy then wrap around the
   mummy. Continue until the whole
   thing is wrapped

4. Cut the end of the string and tape
   on to the back of the mummy

Word Search

HENRY'S ALREADY PLANNING HIS COSTUME FOR NEXT HALLOWEEN. CAN YOU FIND ALL OF HIS IDEAS?

Z	X	Y	N	M	I	E	O	R	T	E	Y	D
N	V	G	Z	O	D	Z	G	V	J	R	K	B
T	S	O	H	G	T	R	F	X	Q	I	Z	I
J	Y	D	W	D	O	E	V	P	V	P	D	F
D	M	I	P	Z	O	R	L	A	C	M	F	Q
J	Q	U	B	G	E	K	L	E	F	A	S	I
E	A	H	M	T	Z	I	N	I	K	V	C	M
F	L	Z	S	M	E	H	Q	D	I	S	L	I
J	H	N	A	N	Y	F	F	S	K	L	O	W
E	O	Z	Z	O	M	B	I	E	Y	T	W	L
M	H	V	Y	R	T	I	A	W	B	Z	N	T
F	L	O	W	E	R	E	W	V	P	A	R	F
J	F	V	U	V	S	C	B	F	H	L	C	C

ALIEN   CLOWN   GHOST

MONSTER   MUMMY   SKELETON

VAMPIRE   WEREWOLF   ZOMBIE

Shadow Puppets

ONE OF THE BEST THINGS ABOUT
HALLOWEEN IS THAT ALL OF
HENRY'S FAVOURITE SHOWS HAVE
HALLOWEEN SPECIALS. THIS TIME
HE'S SO INSPIRED HE'S DECIDED
TO MAKE HIS OWN SHOW WITH
SHADOW PUPPETS.

You will need:

Card	Sticks
Tape	A pencil
Scissors	A torch

Instructions:

1. Draw the outline of a spooky character on a
   piece of card. Great options include witches
   on broomsticks, spiders and bats.

2. Cut out the puppet

3. Use tape to secure a stick to the back of the card

4. Shine a torch on a wall and wave your puppet in front of it to make the shadow

ANSWERS

Trick or Treat

Maze

Word Search

Z	X	Y	N	M	I	E	O	R	T	E	Y	D
N	V	G	Z	O	D	Z	G	V	J	R	K	B
T	S	O	H	G	T	R	F	X	Q	I	Z	I
J	Y	D	W	D	O	E	V	P	V	P	D	F
D	M	I	P	Z	O	R	L	A	C	M	F	Q
J	Q	U	B	G	E	K	L	E	F	A	S	I
E	A	H	M	T	Z	I	N	I	K	V	C	M
F	L	Z	S	M	E	H	Q	D	I	S	L	I
J	H	N	A	N	Y	F	F	S	K	L	O	W
E	O	Z	Z	O	M	B	I	E	Y	T	W	L
M	H	V	Y	R	T	I	A	W	B	Z	N	T
F	L	O	W	E	R	E	W	V	P	A	R	F
J	F	V	U	V	S	C	B	F	H	L	C	C

COLLECT ALL THE
HORRID HENRY STORYBOOKS!